# BEARS MAKE DENS

BY ELIZABETH RAUM   ILLUSTRATED BY ROMINA MARTÍ

AMICUS ILLUSTRATED and AMICUS INK are published by Amicus
P.O. Box 1329, Mankato, MN 56002
www.amicuspublishing.us

LIBRARY OF CONGRESS CATALOGING-IN-PUBLICATION DATA
Names: Raum, Elizabeth, author. | Martí, Romina, illustrator.
Title: Bears make dens / by Elizabeth Raum ; illustrated by Romina Martí.
Description: Mankato, Minnesota : Amicus, [2018] | Series: Animal builders |
    Series: Amicus illustrated | Audience: K to grade 3.
Identifiers: LCCN 2016050069 (print) | LCCN 2017003874 (ebook) |
    ISBN 9781681511719 (library binding) | ISBN 9781681521527 (paperback) |
    ISBN 9781681512617 (e-book)
Subjects: LCSH: Black bear—Juvenile literature. | Bears—Juvenile literature.
Classification: LCC QL737.C27 R384 2018 (print) | LCC QL737.C27 (ebook) |
    DDC 599.78/5—dc23
LC record available at https://lccn.loc.gov/2016050069

EDITOR: Rebecca Glaser
DESIGNER: Kathleen Petelinsek

Printed in the United States of America
HC 10 9 8 7 6 5 4 3 2 1
PB 10 9 8 7 6 5 4 3 2 1

## ABOUT THE AUTHOR

As a child, Elizabeth Raum hiked through the Vermont woods searching for signs that animals lived nearby. She read every animal book in the school library. She now lives in North Dakota and writes books for young readers. Many of her books are about animals. To learn more, go to: elizabethraum.net

## ABOUT THE ILLUSTRATOR

Romina Martí is an illustrator who lives and works in Barcelona, Spain, where her ideas come to life for all audiences. She loves to discover and draw all kinds of creatures from around the planet, who then become the main characters for the majority of her work. To learn more, go to: rominamarti.com

It's spring. A skinny black bear crawls out of its den. Stretch! He's been sleeping all winter.

Now it's time to eat. Fish! Yum! Black bears gain up to 30 pounds (14 kg) a week. They store fat for the next winter.

Black bears find mates, but they do not stay together for long.
Bears are solitary. They usually live alone.

By early fall, bears search for a new den spot.
They will hibernate inside their winter dens.

Papa Bear finds a tall tree with a hollow center.
It will make a fine den.

Mama Bear is still looking. She might choose a crevice in the rocks. Many bears do. This one's too small.

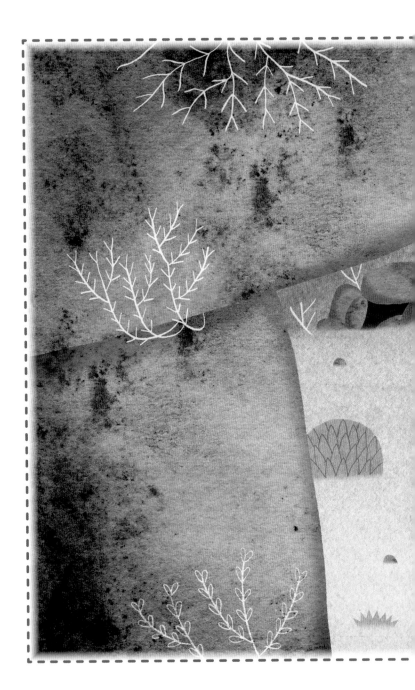

Last year, she found a small cave. It worked well, but she won't use it again. Another bear might use it, though.

Mama Bear finds a fallen tree. It's perfect! She uses her strong front claws to dig a space under the tree. The space is shaped like an egg. It is about 3 feet (1 m) deep and just big enough for one bear.

Mama Bear rakes leaves and twigs into the den to make a cozy bed. Come winter, she'll roll into a tight ball with her head between her big forepaws. The den is ready for winter.

14

The den is not much warmer than the outside air. Mama Bear's fat and thick fur keep her warm. She falls into a deep sleep. Her body slows down. She won't eat or drink until spring.

In January, Mama Bear gives birth. She wakes up just long enough to lick the cubs clean. Then she falls back to sleep.

The tiny cubs have little hair. They snuggle up to Mama Bear to keep warm and to drink her milk. The den keeps them safe all winter.

It's spring! Time to leave the den. Bears wake up slowly. They've been in their dens for three to seven months!

Mama Bear will teach her cubs to find food
and water. They'll eat and play all summer.

When fall comes, the bears look for new dens. The cubs spend one more winter with their mom. Next year, they will make their own dens.

# Where American Black Bears Live

MAP KEY

Where American black bears live

# Build Like a Bear

Bears build dens in tight spaces. Try building your own "den" with a box.

## WHAT BEARS USE

Small, open area in rocks or under a tree

Their claws

Leaves and twigs

## WHAT YOU NEED

Large box, about 3 ft. x 3 ft. (1m x 1m)

Packing tape

Scissors

Blankets and pillows

## WHAT YOU DO

1. Use packing tape to seal the box so it won't open.

2. Cut a hole in the side of the box. The hole should begin at the floor and be big enough to crawl through.

3. Put blankets and pillows inside to make a cozy bed.

4. Crawl into your den for a long winter's nap!

# GLOSSARY

**crevice**  A narrow opening in something, such as a rock or hillside.

**fat**  A source of energy that comes from meat, fish, seeds, and dark leafy plants.

**forepaws**  A bear's powerful front paws.

**hibernate**  To spend the winter sleeping in order to survive cold temperatures and lack of food.

**mate**  The male or female partner of a pair of animals, who join together to breed young.

**solitary**  Living alone, not in families or groups.

# READ MORE

Alinsky, Shelby. *Sleep, Bear!* Washington, D.C.: National Geographic, 2015.

Borgert-Spaniol, Megan. *Grizzly Bears*. Minneapolis: Bellwether Media, 2015.

Brett, Jeannie. *Wild About Bears*. Watertown, Mass.: Charlesbridge, 2014.

Gagne, Tammy. *Black Bears*. Mankato, Minn.: Amicus, 2016.

# WEBSITES

**American Black Bear**

*http://www.nationalgeographic.com/animals/mammals/a/american-black-bear*

See photos and watch videos of bears.

**Brown Bear**

*http://kids.nationalgeographic.com/animals/brown-bear/*

Find photos and basic facts about brown bears.

**"Hungry as a Bear"**

*https://www.nwf.org/Kids/Ranger-Rick/Animals/Mammals/Black-Bears.aspx*

Read about black bears with Ranger Rick.

*Every effort has been made to ensure that these websites are appropriate for children. However, because of the nature of the Internet, it is impossible to guarantee that these sites will remain active indefinitely or that their contents will not be altered.*